NICHOLAS DAY

<u>TABLE OF CONTENTS</u>

PART 1:
SUMMER'S END

I.

R isk existed in the collapsing space between lips just before a
kiss and the banks of the Mischief River were a cemetery to
all that the currents no longer wanted. Homecoming fireworks
exploded through the chill autumnal air, like chants in the tongue
of thunder, violent rainbows that looked of the heavens but stank
of sulfur, crackling light reflected across cold black waters, and
fireworks exploded. People from the little city of October,
Illinois, gathered here at the end of every September, as did the
casual monsters and the invisible ghosts, and so did the great
beast, unseen, who patrolled black waters, here they gathered,
but their ceremonies were not the same. And the beast was not
greedy; only a few would be chosen. Fireworks exploded.

Elizabeth Batson, Lizzie Bat to her friends, a senior at October
High School, she gazed at the technicolor display and listened to
the drifting static as the shower of light wilted, a dying electric
flower. Another bloom erupted in the fertile darkness and its
explosion whispered across the fine hairs on her arms. Her eyes
lost focus and she daydreamed of floating through an outer space
awash in sunsets and sunrises, thunderous chants whispered
across fine hair, all the light in all directions falling and
twinkling, a universe of broken glass. She searched for father's
face amongst the celestial blur. Lizzie Bat remembered there is
no air in outer space, so she fell back to Earth, to the riverbank,
to the black waters, to the grief she buried in the cemetery at the

bottom of her heart.

Fireworks exploded.

"Are you crying?" said Owl.

"I can't do this anymore," said Lizzie Bat, and she said it again, "I can't do this anymore."

Owl, long-suffering, Lizzie Bat's best friend and confidant. The two had lived across the street from one another since they were little girls, and were rarely sighted apart. But an intangible distance grew between them, these days, a dark and terrible shadow cast by grief. Lizzie Bat's heart ached for her father. Owl's heart ached for Lizzie Bat.

"It's no use, Owl," said Spider. "Bats couldn't open up if she was a window."

Spider, perpetually behind his friends—both figuratively and literally—wasn't one to mince words, though he never meant to hurt their feelings. What he lacked in tact, he made up for in loyalty, because he had been brought up to believe love and loyalty were one and the same. And he wasn't one to tolerate bullies, which was evident in his bruises and his scars, not all of which you could see. Spider had his secrets, and he kept them.

Owl raised a fist. "One of these days, buddy."

"No offense," said Spider. "As always."

Lizzie looked over her shoulder. "None taken," she said, and then flipped him off and grinned. "As always," she said.

"I know the fireworks meant a lot to your dad, but don't beat yourself up," said Kat. "We can leave if it's too much. If you start crying, then I'll start crying, then it'll be Owl crying. We'll all look like a gang of raccoons."

Kat, adored, the newest member of the group, though she'd been around just shy two years. She grew up in California, but moved to Illinois with her father after her parents' divorce. Of the four, only Kat possessed both license and car. The red convertible Mustang had been a birthday gift from her mother.

Spider cleared his throat and put a hand to his chest. "Well, I don't wear mascara, but I love garbage," he said. "So, this raccoon votes for drive-thru."

Fireworks exploded. They meant a lot to her father. The cemetery in her heart twisted, burned her eyes and pained her throat.

"Let's go to the city," said Lizzie Bat. "Let's go try something new."

"Across the river?" Spider scoffed. "But I'm hungry now."

"Lizzie wants to leave," said Owl. "Lizzie always wants to leave."

"There's nothing here for me," said Lizzie Bat.

"Oh." Owl wilted like a dying flower. "Thanks for letting me know I'm nothing."

Crackling light reflected across black waters.

"I didn't mean it like that."

Owl looked to Spider and to Kat. "See you at the car," she said, and then retreated through the crowd.

"Wait up," said Spider. He whipped around to Lizzie Bat and said, "Good job." And then, he dissolved into the crowd, too.

The crowd, the chants, the ceremonies, celebration and devastation. Lizzie Bat buried her cemetery heart a little deeper. Many people stood at the banks of the black water, parents with their squirming children, young women like herself, and men, hair up and hair down and in braids and some with no hair at all, young and old, and everyone reflected the violent rainbows exploding overhead, everyone waiting for the chants to whisper across their fine hairs, everyone spread out and down the length of the Mischief River, waiting, everyone waiting, and Lizzie understood that each of them contained their very own cemeteries, buried hearts threatening to break the surface. Fireworks exploded and all these people bloomed, a field of many flowers, bloomed and beautiful, everyone, the crowd, this breathtaking cemetery and its ceremony, devastation and celebration, and everyone waiting for the chants.

Lizzie rolled her eyes and let her shoulders droop. "I ruin everything," she said to Kat.

Kat held out a hand and smiled. She pulled Lizzie Bat to her, turned her around and pointed up. "Two more firecrackers," said Kat. "One for your dad, and one just for us." Lizzie rested her head on Kat's shoulder and Kat put an arm around her friend.

"Thanks," said Lizzie Bat. "I just feel like a ghost, sometimes."

"We all do," said Kat. "But you're our ghost. Remember that."

"Does that mean I get to haunt your house?" said Lizzie Bat. "Remember that."

The black sky cracked and in the very next moment a sea of

red shimmered for Lizzie Bat's father. Red had been his favorite color. And Lizzie allowed herself a hint of a smile, both mourning his absence while being thankful for his memory. The cemetery rested within and Lizzie Bat felt at ease.

"What's that perfume?" asked Lizzie Bat.

"Lavender," said Kat. "I got it at the mall."

"I love it." Lizzie's fingers brushed against Kat's wrist, and Kat took hold of Lizzie's hand.

"I like lavender," said Kat. "It reminds me of my mother."

Rockets whistled to their heights and the fireworks burst near simultaneous, their invisible waves rushed the onlookers who gasped in awe of the purple and green hearts. But Kat and Lizzie Bat did not see the titanous figures hovering over the wide river. They saw only each other.

The crowd ceased to exist and Lizzie Bat floated in outer space, once more, now carried by a green and purple supernova, and she was not alone this time. The constellation before her shouldn't exist, felt somehow impossible. But an invisible wall, some treacherous forcefield, kept her from getting any closer. Risk existed in that collapsing space.

An older boy in the crowd watched them and, once Lizzie noticed his gaze, she remembered there was no air in outer space. She fell back to earth, to riverbank and black waters. But the constellation remained and, unlike the crowd, the constellation kept her bloom and her beautiful colors, a single electric flower in a sea of cemeteries.

"We should go," said Lizzie Bat.

The constellation looked over her shoulder at the boy ogling them. Kat turned towards Lizzie and crinkled her nose. "What a creep," Kat said, and laughed.

Fireworks exploded.

They hurried away from the riverbank and up the grassy slope to the loose gravel where row after row of cars waited patiently. Windshields reflected fireworks and for brief moments it was as if someone shined a great light upon the dusty lot. The spaces between parked cars echoed the pleasures of the crowd. The girls maneuvered through the automobiles like mice in a maze.

"Who was that weirdo?" said Kat.

"Graduated two years ago," said Lizzie Bat. "Lawrence Ragsdale, used to tell everyone he was a vampire."

"Mister popular, I guess."

"Didn't matter. He had a ton of money. His parents own Trick R Treats."

"The Halloween store? It's only open, like, one month out of the year."

"October's claim to fame is being the most haunted city in the country. You've seen how busy Trick R Treats gets. People here go apeshit for Halloween."

"Maybe I should get a job there. Save up some money for Spring Break."

"He'd be your manager, you know. You'd be better off robbing the place."

"He can't be that bad."

"He only hires girls. I hear stories, Kat. For all I know, he really is a vampire."

Spider and Owl were leaning over the trunk of the Mustang, sharing a cigarette and talking to each other in hushed tones. Kat apologized for their taking too long as she unlocked the car. Owl sat in the passenger seat; she liked being in charge of the radio. Spider laid across the back, his head in Lizzie Bat's lap, and he begged for French fries. Lizzie, lost in thought, said nothing. Instead of outer space, she found herself inside Trick R Treats. She was not greedy; it wouldn't take too much money to start life somewhere else, to become a real ghost.

Lizzie Bat whispered, "I can't do this anymore."

The last of the fireworks exploded. And, just like that, homecoming was over and summer was officially dead. The Season of Falling Leaves had arrived.

II.

Reading father's book had been forbidden. Maybe when you're older, he had told her. Maybe never, said her mother, and she meant what she said.

Lizzie Bat waited all the same, waited for the day she would be old enough, bold enough, waited for her mother to forget about the book, waited to revel in the reveal of father's secrets, waited in that way like many others who have waited, waited for a meaning or a purpose to appear, waited for revelation, clarity and clear, waited for her chance, but in the end she simply waited.

And then, Daniel Batson disappeared.

Father had been gone a year when the storage shed, which contained all the copies of the book he had written, father's forbidden book, caught fire during the night. Two-thousand books reduced to ash, Lizzie Bat cried at the sight, her father's second death. Never would she be old enough to see secrets in this smoke and the rest of life yawned out before her, an unfathomable reechy darkness where secrets stretched their skeletal remains across a graveyard with no end. Lizzie Bat, in that moment, wished to never wait, never wait again.

She ran a hand through his carbonized dreams and searched in vain for a single page or a surviving word. Mother shed not a tear. Maybe never, said her mother, and she meant what she said.

"Forget about the book," said mother. "Only witches can read dust, and you're no witch."

"You would know," said Lizzie Bat.

Mother struck her for that. An open palm across the face. The woman may as well have cast a spell; form and features changed from that of mother to a nameless stranger. Lizzie Bat did not know this doppelgänger before her, as if shadow and skin had swapped places.

"He never should've written that damned book," this shadow mother had said on more than one occasion.

Pure luck, it would seem, reared its head in the following weeks. A single copy of father's book, packed and forgotten in the attic, presented itself to Lizzie Bat. What of his clothes remained, and of his childhood things, were stowed up above, out of sight and out of mind and in that way the attic became a kind of hidden museum. Mother demanded his things be left alone, demanded Lizzie Bat dig a grave in her heart and bury her father in it, demanded secrets be secret and to engage in a forgetting.

But up snuck Lizzie Bat, in a secret of her own, and she poured through father's belongings. The hidden museum being as close to heaven as she could get, and closer than his grave, which sat empty, anyway. A body was never found.

Lizzie Bat came home very late, after the fireworks and fast food and late conversations with her friends. She apologized to Owl for hurt feelings. They shared a cigarette in the darkness before saying goodnight, the ember lobbed back and forth, burning bright only to dim again, from lips to lips, like a casual ritual meant to ward off the world of adults for just a little longer, as if every drag captured an extra moment or two in the lungs before being released in a plume of smoke, a little more youth lost in the ether. Distant chimes struck midnight.

Lizzie Bat snuck in through the back of the house, closed the door, and listened for her mother. And listened for her mother. And listened.

Lizzie Bat listened for a step, or a breath, or a mutter, listened to her own heart beat, and beat, and beat.

…

beat beat

…

beat beat

...

beat beat

...

She walked as softly as she could, walking like a whisper would, softly, save her beating heart, the drumming in her ears, barely allowing herself to take anything but the smallest breath for fear of giving up the ghost. Even thoughts were in whispers. And every creak of the floor agonized her more, a tremulous sensation, through her lower back like a chill from an unwanted advance, or a glance from a vampire at a fireworks display. She crept up stairs on hands and feet and wished so much for wings.

She stood in the hall and listened a little while longer.

...

beat beat

...

beat beat

...

beat beat

...

Finally, she reached up, opened the hatch, and lowered the ladder. Up to heaven where the secret museum lay before her in a dozen or so boxes. She held one of his shirts to her nose and allowed herself quiet tears.

A red scarf lay folded in the very same box. He had worn that red scarf every winter, and judging by photo albums—much older than herself—he had worn the red scarf even as a very young man. Had he purchased the red scarf or had the red scarf been a gift or passed on to him by another relative? Lizzie Bat never gave the red scarf a single thought before, but now she desperately wished to know the red scarf's secrets.

Much of his voice slipped away over time. But she could close her eyes and hear him say her name, say her name and the little things he'd say through the day. And she thought of all the times she didn't respond or rolled her eyes instead of telling him how much she loved him.

Hey there, Lizzie Bat.

"Hi, dad."

Hey, squirt, how's my lady?

"I wish you were here."

Pop a squat, kiddo!

"I wish you were here." (her body shook)

Stay awhile, talk to the old man.

"I wish you were here." (her shoulders shook)

I didn't want anything.

"I wish you were here." (her chest shook)

I love you, Lizzie Bat, I hope you know that.

She pressed her palms to her eyes and hoped she would stop crying, hoped that pain could be captured, hoped but hoped in vain. Lizzie Bat shook and cried as silently as her body would allow, and when her body finished, she collected herself and wiped her eyes.

She reached into the box and then wrapped the red scarf around her neck. And that's when she spied, poking out from between more clothes, the corner of a book. She held her breath.

No dust jacket. No title or author name, neither on the cover nor the spine, leant the book an air of mystery. Lizzie Bat was one to indulge curiosity, and so she tried to open the tome but binding popped and cracked in objection to this violation, as if these words were not meant for her. The book wished to remain closed and to be forgotten. But, Lizzie Bat would never wait again, so she wrenched open the stubborn cover and the spine crackled like cackling laughter. Her eyes widened.

This was his book.

His words.

His voice.

She could *hear* him.

And as she turned the pages, he spoke to her.

HALLOWEEN
FOREVER

A Memoir

DANIEL BATSON

"Love each other or perish."
—Auden

Copyright © 1997 by Daniel Batson

PUBLISHED BY RIVERBEND PRESS
MISCHIEF, ILLINOIS

MANUFACTURED IN THE UNITED STATES OF AMERICA

*To Lizzie B
With all my love & hope for
your future.
You are the best of two worlds,
Above and Below.*

PROLOGUE

First, cryptid is just a word for a creature that doesn't exist. Now, a fancy pants will use the term unsubstantiated, but some of our greatest philosophers have called into question the very existence of reality, so I guess that makes us all just a little unsubstantiated. You only know what you think you know, and for some folks that's good enough. But knowing what you know was never good enough for me. I went looking.

Second, my grandpa, who came to live with mama and I after papa got killed, he wouldn't be caught dead using a term like unsubstantiated. He was not a fancy pants, a fact he was all too happy to share after a loud burp or a sonorous fart. Nor did he call them cryptids, which wasn't even a word until 1983. Grandpa called them October Animals, and that is what I call them and that is what I am, and what you are.

Third, I can't say that I set out to kill anyone, though I didn't carry that rifle with me for shits and grins. Searching for monsters can be dangerous. I was going to use it, if it came to that. And if you have a gun and a head full of anger, then chances are that it will come to that. I remember my high school English teacher. She went on and on about empathy, how you could really learn empathy by reading a book. But you know what? When your head is packed with hurt and your heart is in anguish, you think you can teach empathy with a gun. At least, that's what you believe in the moment. You're hurt. You're looking to make somebody else hurt. That's the way of stupid beasts. There is no magic in violence.

Fourth, the cliché is that you never really know a person, but the reality is that you never really know your self. You only know what you think you know, and you don't even really know that. And you can go looking, like I did, but all you are going to find out there is October Animals. Some are more dangerous than others. Some of them are hiding in the woods, hiding in the caves, hiding at the bottom of deep waters, and some yet roam the deserts of the West, but some are in the mirror if you look hard enough. I went looking.

And this is what I found.

"Elizabeth Rae Batson." Shadow Mother called from the hallway down below. "Get out of that attic this instant."

The woman stomped twice, stomped twice, on the hardwood floor and Lizzie Bat dropped his forbidden book in panic. But Shadow Mother hadn't seen her, hadn't seen her, neither did she see the book, the forbidden, the red scarf, she hadn't seen her, hadn't seen anything at all.

Lizzie Bat wrapped father's red scarf around her neck. She picked up the book and then tucked it under her shirt and in the waist of her jeans. Shadow Mother had not touched her in a spell, since *the* spell, had not touched her since the fire, and his red scarf would surely keep the doppelgänger's attention and, Lizzie Bat hoped, the doppelgänger's ire.

"Jesus, mom, you gave me a heart attack," she said, buying time.

"You have no business digging through his things," said Shadow Mother. "Digging through his things is not safe."

Lizzie Bat hurried down the ladder.

"I'm sorry," said Lizzie Bat. "I won't do it again."

Shadow Mother raised her hand, raised her features, an accusatory glare, pointed not at Lizzie Bat but at the red scarf around her neck. "Take that"—and here she raised her voice —"off."

"No."

"Would you like to change your tune, young lady?"

"You can keep all of it, I don't care." Lizzie Bat gripped the red scarf. "But this is mine."

"None of this is yours, do you hear me? I will burn it all. I will burn it tomorrow."

"That's your answer to everything."

"I am not your enemy. I do not want you getting hurt."

"Nothing up there is going to hurt me. You're acting crazy."

"I am trying to keep you safe."

"Safe from what?"

"I do not want you ending up like your father."

"You lied to the police. Lied to me. You know, don't you?"

"He never should have written that book. He never should have gone looking."

"Looking for what?"

I went looking.

"Stay out of the attic. Stay out of his things."

"What are you so afraid of?"

"Stay out of the attic. Stay out of his things."

"What do you think I am going to find?"

I went looking.

Shadow Mother gripped Lizzie Bat's arm. "Death."

A chill ran up Lizzie Bat's back and both arms tingled with gooseflesh. "I can't do this anymore." She pulled away. "I'm going to bed," she said. "I'm locking the door." Tears welled in her eyes but she would not cry in front of this thing. "I can't do this anymore."

"Yes," said Shadow Mother. "Lock your door. Turn off the light."

Lizzie Bat drifted backwards down the dark hall and locked herself in her bedroom. She tucked his forbidden book under her pillow, kicked off her jeans, and then crawled under her covers. Sleep arrived, soon enough, but no dreams waited, only deeper and darker things.

So, at an odd hour, Lizzie Bat awoke, unable to remember what had disturbed her so. She reached up and felt his red scarf around her neck and she took a heavy breath. Red light flashed from atop the dresser across the room, the digital clock blinking as if there had been a power outage, but the lamp on her bedside table turned on without a problem.

The door to her room stood open.

"Oh no," she said. "Oh no."

Lizzie Bat put a hand beneath her pillow. She cried out, tossed the pillow aside, pulled back her sheets. And then, she scrambled to the floor and looked beneath her bed. His book, his words, his voice.

Gone.

A smell, a memory, like carbonized dreams and words turned to ash, tore through her senses. A fire burned nearby. And, Lizzie Bat went looking.

III.

Shadow Mother stood before an early-morning bonfire in the middle of their backyard. A cigarette hung lazily from her mouth, the smoldering tip a red beauty mark that hummed in the dark outline of her face. Her thin silhouette bisected the flames behind her which rose in sharp tongues and licked the air and roared like continuous thunder. Bright embers crackled and cackled, a litany of harsh whispers, burned like a cast spell, crackled and cackled.

The fire on either side of Shadow Mother gave her wings, the wings of something you'd find in Hell. And the shadows cast danced in glee, danced and reached for Lizzie Bat to join in the reverie. All the shadows cast by the fire danced in celebration, danced the dance of devastation, danced in reverie. And the embers crackled and cackled.

The fire whipped about as if it had hands, long fingered, bright and searching for someone to thrash, to grab, to pull into itself and feed. Risk existed in the darkness between mother and child. Lizzie Bat would wait no more and she balled her fist and she dared move forward, but froze.

Shadow Mother held a scythe as if she were death. "Don't come any closer," she said.

Crackle and cackle.

Birdsong echoed in the stillness of pre-dawn. They called to the sun and it would come. Witches on feathered wings.

Lizzie Bat was flush with anger, a burning ember that shone brightly in the dark, eager to become her own fire and flame, eager for wings, ready to render this woman before her to ash and a forgetting.

"What are you doing?" said Lizzie Bat. "What have you done?"

"Forget about the book," said Shadow Mother. "Only witches can read dust, and you're no witch."

Fire crackled like cackling laughter. Lizzie Bat's eyes widened.

His book.

His words.

His voice.

She could *hear* him.

"Am I not your daughter?" said Lizzie Bat. "Am I not a witch, like you?"

"I am no mere witch," Shadow Mother said.

Shadow Mother slammed the scythe into the earth so that it stood on its own and at an odd angle. She regarded her daughter for several silent moments, finished her cigarette, then dropped the butt and grinded it beneath her heal. She never looked away from the young woman. Shadow Mother walked across the lawn, closing the distance, the darkness between them tightening and coiling like a snake, until they were clothed in the very same shadow, not dancing like the other shadows, but oh so still, until the two women were eye to eye, until their darkness was one and the same. Crackle and cackle.

Sun threatened to crest the horizon.

"I have a struggle within me," Shadow Mother said. The words escaped her in a whisper accompanied by tendrils of smoke and she looked, briefly, like a dragon. "I wish to be, to do, good. I want to stave off despair. But there *is* something else. I would become as a cloud. I would rise up, a black mass of choking ash . . . and you would look upon me, and I would lie down upon the Earth like a stream. And all of you, as still as the pebbles and the rocks below. I would wear you down to sand and then scatter you like a distant memory."

Lizzie Bat said, "Smoking is bad for you."

Shadow Mother swooped toward her, a predator descending from the clouds. She stood tall and rail thin, with amber eyes and silver hair. Not grey, but silver, hairs spun out of fine, metal strands, regal and cut in the pageboy style, like Audrey Hepburn's evil twin or a dragon who wanted very much to become a human, a nameless stranger. Lizzie Bat did not know this doppelgänger, and risk existed in the collapsing space between them.

"Do you want to strike me?" Shadow Mother said. "As I struck you?"

"Don't say anything that you might regret."

Shadow Mother placed her hand to Lizzie Bat's cheek. "Dear child, I've never regretted anything I've ever said before, and I don't think I ever will. There are times, and maybe you're feeling this right now, but often it is what is left *unsaid* that is the biggest regret of them all." Shadow Mother smiled at her. "Am I right? Are you feeling that kind of regret right now?"

"I can't do this anymore," said Lizzie Bat. "I hate you."

"Strike me," said Shadow Mother. "Raise that soft fist and strike me down."

"I'll kill you."

"Violence is a spell that we cast on one another," said Shadow Mother. "Cast your spell on me."

"There is no magic in violence," said Lizzie Bat. "That's the way of stupid beasts."

Shadow Mother smacked Lizzie Bat across the face and she stumbled backwards. Her skin burned and eyes watered. Crackled and cackled. For a brief moment, she swore Shadow Mother bared her teeth, like an animal, and like an animal those teeth were *sharp*.

"You will not use his words against me," said Shadow Mother.

Birds who sang like morning bells had cast their spell successfully and conjured sun and dark and blue all washed away, dancing shadows, reverie, all retreated, ran away. Lizzie Bat, now defeated, also retreated, and ran away. Shadow Mother called to her.

Lizzie Bat ran on and wondered where her grave would be. She ran and wondered where her grave waited like an opened mouth with a hunger only for her, her rot and ruin its one and only meal. She ran and wondered if she ran to her grave this very minute.

Lizzie Bat conjured up a headstone, what it said, a name, a

birth, a day that she would die, and a dash or a cross that would separate these dates, a dash or a cross that represent all the days she lived between, all the days one spent living, all the days that were a struggle, all the days in those symbols, symbols small, but so are days, days that felt important when in fact most are the same, and in the end only two of those days remain, while the rest are just condensed to a symbol beneath your name, a simple symbol, and two dates, and above all that a name. Perhaps the most important thing about the stone atop your grave is the people who will come and stop and read and mourn your name.

She ran and wondered.

Spider with his secrets, he would show his face. Owl would mourn, of course she would, but she would also be resentful and complain she'd been left behind. And then, there was Kat, the lovely constellation who smelled of lavender and felt like risk.

Lizzie Bat did not run to her grave that morning. She ran to her friends. She ran to her October Animals.

IV.

Clear morning had become an afternoon shadowed by a stretch of grey cloud. No breeze amongst the trees lining the lonely park and no breeze down below where the grass did grow. A single gazebo stood at the park's center. This is where Lizzie Bat gathered her friends.

Thick, cool air that tasted electric poured across Lizzie Bat's skin and sent her hair into wild spasms. She closed her eyes and smiled because she loved the smell of rain, and rain was coming. Of that, she was sure, and she hoped the storm would wash the town away.

"I'm leaving on Halloween night," she told them.

Lizzie Bat looked up and tried to cast a spell and called to the rain and begged the rain to come. She thought of the birds and their wings and how the sun rose for their call and her heart yearned for wings and magic but Shadow Mother was right. Lizzie Bat could not read dust. Nor did she possess wings. No spells to cast. No magic. The clouds looked very much like rolling waves and she felt like a creature at the bottom of the sea who dreamed of escape. And, sooner than later, long days would end and the sun would ensconce itself completely and the Midwest would wrap up in a chrysalis of grey cloud and misery. She was powerless and adrift at the thought.

"I can't do this anymore," she said. "If I stay here, then I will kill my mother or she will kill me."

"That's fucked up," said Spider.

"She burned my father's things," said Lizzie Bat. "She burned the only copy of his book. She hit me, again. And she's changing."

"Is there anywhere you can go?" said Spider.

"There's a grave waiting for me like an open mouth," said Lizzie Bat. "I've seen it."

"It's been a hard year," said Owl. "For you and your mom. But it won't be this way forever."

"People love to say it's been a hard year, as if life isn't just one long fucking year," said Lizzie Bat. "You're born, it's January, and it stays that way until you're dead."

"Always the optimist," said Spider.

"Optimism is an evolutionary safeguard against reality," said Kat.

Lizzie Bat smiled. "She gets it."

"We all get it, you sour ass," said Spider.

"Life is shit," said Owl. "It's practically your mantra."

"I'm not joking." Lizzie Bat turned to face her friends. "I'm leaving," she said. "And I am never coming back."

"You can't just leave," said Owl.

"Goddamnit." Lizzie Bat marched right up to Owl and pushed her. "Stop telling me that."

Owl threw out her arms. "Where will you go?" she said. "You don't even have a car."

Lizzie Bat shot a glance to Kat before turning back to Owl.

"She is going to kill me," said Lizzie Bat. "It doesn't matter where I go as long as it's far away from my mother."

Owl crossed her arms. "With what money?"

"It wouldn't take much money to start life somewhere else," said Lizzie Bat. "I could ghost this place for next to nothing."

"Nothing." Owl didn't miss a beat. "That's about how much you have."

"I *have* to leave," said Lizzie Bat. She pointed at Owl. "But you don't have to stay."

Owl had no comeback. She looked to Kat and Spider who both clearly waited for her retort. "I don't have to stay," Owl whispered. She took out a cigarette and fumbled with her lighter.

Lizzie Bat stepped towards Owl. "You don't have to stay," said Lizzie Bat, realizing the power of those words. "You don't have to stay."

"Stop saying that." Owl shook too much to light her cigarette.

"You don't have to stay."

"I said *stop*."

The lighter slipped through Owl's fingers and bounced and landed at Lizzie Bat's feet. Lizzie Bat dropped to her knees. She held the lighter in her hand and offered it to Owl.

"You don't have to stay," Lizzie Bat said, and then, she finished her first spell. "Come with me."

Owl, who lived across the street and whose heart ached, felt an intangible distance close between she and her best friend. Rarely were they sighted apart and now it could be that way forever and always. Her suffering seemed to grow wings and fly away. She took the lighter and the tips of her fingers brushed Lizzie Bat's palm but it felt much deeper than skin and Owl did not know it but she fell inside of Lizzie Bat, who had her, now, and kept her in a place like dreams but deeper and somehow darker.

"I don't have to stay," said Owl.

The sky thundered and rain fell.

"We're going to leave on Halloween night," Lizzie Bat said to Owl. "We're going to rob Trick R Treats and then we are going to use that money to disappear from this place."

Lizzie Bat closed her eyes. She smiled and felt electric.

Downpour soaked the October Animals and the four of them took shelter under the gazebo. Lightning refused to strike but curled and spread in splintered webs, like shattering glass, across the bottom of the rolling clouds. The air smelled sweet, tasted metallic, and seemed to howl from all directions at once. Lizzie Bat wondered if the lightning waited for her invitation. She had invited the rain, after all, but not the lightning. She very much appreciated the patience of lightning.

"Owl is with me," she said to Spider and Kat.

And Spider and Kat looked at one another.

"You're asking us to commit a crime," said Spider. "Probably *multiple* crimes."

"I'm in," said Kat.

"Oh, wow." Spider shook his head. "Just like that?" he asked. "Just wait for me to open my mouth and then throw me under the bus. Very nice."

Lizzie Bat walked to and hugged Spider. "Thank you," she

said.

Spider laughed. "You're, uh… welcome?" Spider, caught completely off guard, let his arms close around Lizzie Bat very slowly. "Does this mean we aren't commiting crimes?"

Lizzie Bat pulled back and smiled at her friend. She cupped the side of his face. "You are always trying to protect us," she said. "And I will always love you for that."

Kat left Spider's side and stood beside Owl.

"Three against one," said Owl.

"You are always trying to protect us." Lizzie Bat curled a strand of Spider's hair around her finger. "And I will always love you for that."

"You keep saying that and I might just believe you," said Spider.

Spider, perpetually behind his friends—both figuratively and literally—now stood before them. He didn't want to hurt their feelings. He wanted to be loyal and he wanted to be loved. And he would protect them, if he could. He would protect them in the way he so desperately wished someone had protected him, he would protect them from bruises, he would protect them from scars. And if Spider could keep his secrets, then he could keep their secrets, too.

"You are always trying to protect us." Lizzie Bat kissed him on the forehead. "And I will always love you for that."

Spider pushed away from Lizzie Bat, not in anger but in resignation. He couldn't stop the word *love* from playing over and over again, in his head, in her voice. He felt dizzy and leaned on the gazebo railing. The young women all watched and waited.

"Okay," he said, and reached a hand into the rain. "Let's rob Trick R Treats. Let's disappear."

Lightning had waited long enough, and Lizzie Bat knew exactly what to do with it. "Kat, can you take us to my house?" she asked. She looked into the eyes of each of her friends. "Mother will try to stop me if I am alone."

"Stop you from what?" asked Kat.

"From reading dust, of course."

V.

Daniel Batson died, he disappeared and died, and that was just the first time. The second time he died was when his books burned up inside of storage, smouldered and smoked like a soul escaping. Shadow Mother never cried, never cried, thought she could hide behind the flames. And how she changed as she tried to deprive a daughter of her father's dreams. But hope was a rope Lizzie Bat held onto and his book, his words, his voice, found her in his secret things.

Maybe never, said her mother, and she meant what she said.

Daniel Batson died, and then he died, and then he died again.

The remains of Daniel Batson's books and secret things smouldered and smoked, rendered ash by Shadow Mother, then rendered mud by wind and rain. Lizzie Bat tried to read, tried to see, to render mud and ash and smoulder and smoke whole again. Drops of rain pattered her head and snuck through the hair to tickle the scalp and smoke crept into her nose and slid down her throat, pungent and eye-watering, sharp on the back of the tongue.

"There's nothing there worth saving," said Spider. "No offense."

"I am not a witch." She looked over her shoulder at her friends. "I cannot read dust."

I cannot read dust.

I cannot read dust.

I cannot read dust.

Goosebumps flooded her skin. Rain no longer tickled her scalp, but crept up her shoulders and up her neck. Lizzie Bat raised an arm and watched water pull itself together in droplets and fall up into the sky. She wrote her plea on every drop until her body dried from head to toe and where she stood fell not a drop from the sky. She spoke to the clouds above in their very own language.

I cannot read dust.

"Are you two seeing this?" asked Spider. But neither Owl nor Kat said a word.

That sharp taste crept back up Lizzie Bat's throat, all the smoke and smoulder that had settled in her lungs now crawled into her brain and she spoke to smoke like she spoke to clouds above. *I cannot read dust.* She fell to her knees and tears of smoke bled from her eyes, cutting through rain, and reaching into mud. Crackle and cackle, once more, embers born anywhere the smoke touched down, and mud dried and brittled and became as ash, devastation and celebration.

October Animals bore witness in silence. Thunder chanted in response to Lizzie Bat's invocation. Ceremony ended and each of them looked up and waited. Rain stopped. Wind ceased. All the world hushed. No man or animal moved. The song of all living things paused. Even the universe crawled to a stop.

Lightning exploded.

Brilliant and blinding to all but Lizzie Bat. And oh, how the Animals screamed behind her. But they would soon enough see what this witch had wrought. Shadow Mother's funeral pyre had cratered and at its ashen center sat a book made of glass.

His book.

His words.

His voice.

Lizzie Bat opened the glass book. The edge of a page knicked her fingertip and it bloomed. A trickle ran across and settled into a sentence. His voice became crimson.

`I went looking.`

The sound of the back door opening registered only to Owl and Spider and Kat. Lizzie Bat paid no attention to the metrical stomping of matriarchal feet. These sounds meant very little to her, now. Those spells were broken.

"Give that to me," said Shadow Mother.

Lizzie Bat refused to look at the woman. She took the red scarf from her neck and wrapped it around his glass words. She held his voice and scarf to her chest, closed her eyes, and smiled. She loved the smell of rain and, for her, the rain had come. Downpour did not wash away the town as she'd hoped, but rain left her with a gift.

"You told me that you were not my enemy." Lizzie Bat felt her cemetery heart bloom. "But I am yours."

PART 2:
THE SEASON OF FALLING LEAVES

Halloween, 1958

I had seen monsters before, but nothing like the behemoth which crawled out of Mischief River on that Halloween night.

My papa was an alcoholic and my mama was mentally ill. Neither recognized their diseases nor sought treatment. In the 1950's, such things were taboo and only spoken of in whisperers. Easier to shun these types, you see. And, so it was for my family. Mother and father shunned, and I, guilty by association. Childhood, in many ways, was a horror story I do not care to recall. But this book isn't for me, so I'll open up these wounds and you can take a look inside.

October, Illinois, always held Halloween close to its heart. So did I. After all, where we are is who we are. And the children of October have certain, shall we say, expectations hoisted upon them by the community. Understand, other holidays were but a single date on the calendar. But, Halloween? Halloween lasted all the year. Halloween forever! The image of Peter Pumpkin-eater, jack-o-lanterns, black bats and black cats, candy corn, silly spirits, and spiders with light-up eyes. Any day of the year, in the square downtown, you could play a game similar to Pin the Tail on the Donkey. Superstition dictated that the game never be given a name, but there was a rhyme that accompanied it, well-known in and around the city, but nowhere else, really.

> Purple, orange, yellow, black
> I forget where I'm at
> Halloween forever

Players wear a blindfold and stand in the middle of five pumpkins, only one of which has been carved into a jack-o-lantern. After being spun, either on their own accord or with the help of bystanders, the player is given a candle. One chance to pick the right pumpkin, to light the jack-o-lantern. The winner is said to get nothing but treats all year after. Losers, of course, get tricks. This divination game was played over and over by young and old alike. Although, I only played it the once. My parents, maybe never.

A childhood in October is filled, or should be filled, with a multitude of good Halloween memories. Unfortunately, this wasn't the case for me. Papa and mama never took me out trick-or-treating. For a long time, I assumed they simply didn't care for the holiday. I was much older when I had the realization people didn't want us at their homes. We were, I suppose, real monsters, never allowed to take off our masks. In fact, I only went out on Halloween night a single time. Never again.

That particular year saw too many late-summer storms, and the air remained *terribly hot well into the fall. The river had swelled considerably, creeping beyond its banks and threatening houses and businesses downtown. The annual Halloween parade was cancelled, one of only two times in the city's 179 years. The mayor even advised against trick-or-treating, telling people to keep their festivities inside where it would be warm and safe.*

Just before midnight, October 31st, the rain stopped. And it had rained for so long, so persistently, that the sudden silence woke me from a deep slumber. There was a light knocking on the bedroom door and papa let himself into my room. He asked if I wanted to go out and look at the swollen Mischief River. The moon is out, he told me, and the river will look like a thick vein of silver. And maybe some of the jack-o-lanterns will still be lit, he added, if they were out of the rain.

He did not have to ask twice.

I grabbed my black rubber boots and my long yellow raincoat, the raincoat with the matching yellow hat. And then, papa grabbed me, lifted me clean off the floor. He smiled and I hugged him for what would be the last time. He carried me to our truck and put me inside, started up the engine to let it warm. But he didn't sit inside with me. He stood with his back to the headlights and stared out into the darkness beyond their reach, like he heard something or saw something. But I was too excited to really notice, to be afraid.

I turned on the radio and tuned into the local station which was playing nothing but Halloween music. The whole world seemed to hold its breath in anticipation. Clouds parted and stars shone as brightly as I had ever seen them. I hardly noticed papa clamber into the truck.

We backed down the wet, gravel driveway and headed downtown. At the time, I was small enough to stand up on the floor of the truck but tall enough to see over the dash. Empty roads, slick with moonlight. Not a soul outside except us and in the darkness lining the streets blazed jack-o-lanterns, their toothy grins and triangle eyes, the shapes of bats and cats and spiders and skulls. There was even an owl.

Downtown October, at least three or so blocks, sat under the flooded Mischief River. Papa parked well away from the water and we walked the rest of the distance. And he was right, the black waters were painted in silver and stretched on and on into the distance. I asked papa if the ocean looked like this, but he didn't answer me because something upriver caught his eye. Then, he mumbled some such about a levee giving out north of the Chester farm. A popular place this time of year, you could go on hay rides and wander the cornfield maze and for a couple of bucks you could grab one of the pumpkins out of old Mr. Chester's pumpkin patch. We'd never been, but I heard other kids talk about it.

We'd never been but that didn't matter, because on October 31st, 1958, the pumpkin patch came to us. Hundreds of pumpkins came floating down the swollen river, like an invasion. You want to carve a jack-o-lantern, papa asked me, and he marched right down to the river's edge and got in to his knees. He held a wet pumpkin over his head and laughed when it dripped on his hair and then he screamed like I never heard anyone scream. He came down so hard that the pumpkin split open on the pavement.

Papa rolled over and beat at his legs and he seemed to get free because he managed to crawl out of the water. He tried standing but his left leg was gone below the knee and he fell hard. I remember him asking for help over and over and being out of breath and reaching out to me. But I froze solid when I saw that thing rise up above the water behind him. Moonlight offered the barest of details, but they were enough. Horns like a deer and the size of a small car, a turtle's face, only more skull-like, and a heavy beard.

Papa started asking for help again but in his smallest voice and the thing set upon him. The last image I have of my father is the look of surprise as the beast bit into the back of his head and I turned and ran as fast as I could. Jack-o-lanterns watched over me as I went, and the only thought running through my mind was a rhyme. And these words, they seemed to keep me from falling apart, kept me from screaming, held all of reality together in one piece.

Purple, orange, yellow, black
I forget where I'm at
Halloween forever

I.

The Season of Falling Leaves sounds like shuffling feet on hallway floors, the rattle and slam of locker doors, pencils and pens that scribble and scratch, pages turned and pages crinkled. Summer's corpse could be seen in forlorn glances through classroom windows to the world outside, now denied to onlookers. The slow advance of a clock's second hand served as a sermon but offered little hope to mourners watching the minutes pass. Summer always died after homecoming.

And summer's death was felt by both students and teachers. The afternoons may have still been warm and humid, the trees retaining some amount of green, but summer was a freedom and that freedom ended the moment children entered those doors and took their seats. Children no longer but, instead, reduced to students, existing as a single body often at war with itself. The adults, stripped of their lives beyond the classroom door, known only for the subject they taught. School was its own season to be suffered through, hot or cold, rain or shine.

The October Animals did not share many classes, but they all had the same lunch hour, and because they were allowed off campus, their ritual was not to eat but to meet across the street and share cigarettes, tell stories, and dream of seasons that existed only for adults. Lizzie Bat, however, was done dreaming, done waiting. She smiled, and she felt like she could smile forever.

"I want each of you to steal something for me," she said to her friends. "Something only you could steal, but something you'd never dream of taking."

"You're going to get caught," said Owl. "You're going to get caught or hurt or worse."

Lizzie Bat rolled her eyes and said, "I am not getting caught," then blew smoke in Owl's face.

"That's easy," said Spider. He snatched the cigarette from Lizzie's hand. "I know exactly what I'd take."

"So do I," said Kat.

"Isn't robbing Trick R Treats bad enough?" said Owl. "Maybe you don't get caught. But, Spider could get caught, so could Kat."

"You're afraid," said Lizzie Bat. "You've always been afraid of getting in trouble."

"Damn you," Owl said. "How about Spider gets *killed*?"

"That's not fair," said Spider. "Why do I have to be the one who gets killed?"

"Nobody is getting killed," said Lizzie Bat.

"What if Kat gets caught?" said Owl. "What if she gets caught and . . . sent to live with her mother in California?"

Lizzie Bat's smile faded. She locked eyes with Kat for the briefest moment, a pained look drew across Kat's face.

"And suddenly you give a shit." Owl clenched her teeth and sucked in. "I knew it. I fucking *knew* it."

Lizzie Bat felt a tickle in her lower back. She dipped into the pool of black at the bottom of her memories. She gripped a jagged piece of fear and anger and dragged this rot to the surface. Cigarette smoke slowly rolled from her mouth and pooled around her eyes before rising up above her head, twisting and turning like great gray horns. She looked, briefly, like a dragon.

Owl could barely recognize her friend.

"Do you want to strike me?" asked Lizzie Bat.

Owl did not back down. "I'd love to," she said.

"Do it," said Lizzie Bat. "I can take it."

Owl crushed her right hand into a tight fist.

Spider laughed and said, "Maybe you two need to chill out."

"Fuck off, Spider," said Owl, and she swung fast. The blow connected hard and sounded like a loud clap. Spider and Kat winced in unison.

Lizzie Bat stumbled backwards but kept herself from falling over completely, bent forward and balanced with her hands on her knees. Spider and Kat moved as if to help, but Lizzie Bat held out a hand and they didn't take another step. She looked up at Owl. Blood poured out of Lizzie Bat's nose. "Do you feel better?" she said. Her left eye was already swelling and her cheek bruised. Blood dripped from her chin and ran down her neck, over and under her white Nirvana t-shirt. Lizzie Bat stood there looking like she'd been cut into two.

Owl cupped her mouth and began to cry. "Oh my god," she said, repeatedly. "I'm so sorry, I didn't mean to."

"Stop," said Lizzie Bat. "I'm not mad at you."

"They're gonna suspend me," Owl said in a moan. "My mom is gonna freak out."

"You aren't getting suspended." Lizzie Bat held herself upright, as if nothing at all had happened. The distance closed between them, though neither seemed to move. "No one is going to freak out." Lizzie Bat reached out and took Owl by the hand. "You are not going to get in trouble."

"I'm not?" said Owl. She shook her head. "But you're covered in blood. I hit you."

"You are not going to get in trouble," said Lizzie Bat. "I promise." Lizzie Bat kissed the hand that struck her and Owl was hers again. "You are *not* going to get in trouble," she said, and smiled. And she felt like she could smile forever.

"I want each of you to steal something for me," she said to her friends. "Something only you could steal. But something you'd never dream of taking."

"I know the perfect thing," said Owl.

Lizzie Bat held a finger to Owl's lips. "Don't tell me," she said. "Surprise me."

"You know," Spider cleared his throat and continued, "you can't go to class looking like that."

"You look like a horror movie," said Kat.

"I'm not going to class," said Lizzie Bat. "I'm going home."

Kat sighed, then said, "Someone's bound to ask about you."

"Tell them I got sick." Lizzie Bat looked at the blood on her shirt. She grinned. "Tell them I got my period."

The school bell screamed. Owl gave Lizzie Bat a cigarette for the road, and then the October Animals parted ways. Spider and

Kat and Owl did not speak, but thought of the danger ahead, what it was they would steal, and who they were stealing from.

Lizzie Bat did not live close to the school. The walk home would last an hour, at least, but this didn't bother her. The early-autumn day was bright and breezy. The wind carried a hint of burning leaves, of fireplaces, emissaries of the waiting winter months. And, Lizzie Bat knew a rhyme to help pass the time.

"Purple, orange, yellow, black," she whispered. "I forget where I'm at. Halloween forever."

II.

Spider and Lizzie Bat stood across the street from the two-story Victorian home. His parents had inherited the house after Grandpa Whistle died. Spider's mother wanted to sell but Spider's father thought the home could be a rental property. *Easy money*, he had said. They never kept tenants for long and, after awhile, word got around that something was dreadfully wrong with the old Victorian on top of Christian Hill.

"I didn't know you had a second house," said Lizzie Bat.

Spider frowned. "We own it but we don't go in it."

"A bit of a cheat," Lizzie Bat said. "Stealing from yourself."

"There's a reason we don't go inside," said Spider. "A reason why this place sits empty."

"But it's not empty." Lizzie Bat pointed to the second story. "Someone's watching us from that window."

Spider looked down. "Walk over to the house." He kicked at the dead leaves and said, "He'll disappear."

Lizzie Bat hopped off the sidewalk and sauntered across the cobble-stone street. The old man smiled and she made as if to wave but he vanished. There one moment and gone the next. She hadn't even blinked. Lizzie Bat turned to Spider, her mouth hanging open. "You own a haunted house and didn't let us know?"

"I told you." Spider could barely bring himself to look up. "We own it but we don't go in it." Autumn chill ran its fingers across Spider's stomach and arms and he clutched himself and shivered. "Something only I could steal, right?"

"Something you'd never dream of taking," said Lizzie Bat. She turned and looked at the empty second-floor window. "What could you possibly steal from a ghost?"

"I don't even know if it's possible," said Spider. "He always seems to get it back."

Lizzie Bat crooked her mouth and folded her arms. "Not everything has to be a secret."

Trees had lost nearly all their leaves, and Spider thought the bare branches looked like lacerations, like split skin after being hit too hard with a belt. Red and yellow and orange colored what leaves remained, and these were his bruises. Brown leaves blanketed the large lot on either side of the house, hiding the scars of previous seasons.

"There's a glass eye inside that house. Renters almost always mention it, mention throwing it away, only to have it show up again, later. They never stick around long enough to throw it away a second time. But they name the same three places where they find it, over and over. Beside the kitchen sink on the first floor, on the back of the toilet upstairs, and on a shelf in the basement. If I'm lucky, it'll be in the kitchen. That's a straight shot from the front door. In and out."

"And if you're not lucky?"

"I never thought I'd come to this house ever again, never dreamed in a million years I'd walk through those doors without kicking and screaming. I haven't been in that basement since…" Spider fought the pain building in his throat. He swallowed, hard, and tried to shove all the shame he felt back into his stomach. "I was brought up to believe bad people went to Hell when they died." He laughed. "Never pictured Hell as a two-story house with a nice view."

"You don't have to go alone."

Spider whipped around to face her. "Promise me you won't go inside that house," he said. He placed his hands on her shoulders. "No matter what you hear, no matter how bad it sounds."

"Always trying to protect us." Lizzie Bat rested her cheek against his hand and closed her eyes. "I'll always love you for that."

"You are the *only* person in the world who could get me to go in that house."

"Give me one of your secrets before you leave," she said. "I won't ever ask for another, I promise."

Spider's eyes wandered. He looked at everything and nothing, to the sky and to the ground. Finally, he smiled. "I'm in love with Owl," he said. His cheeks blossomed and he laughed a little and shook his head.

"I won't say a word," said Lizzie Bat. "I promise."

"Doesn't matter," Spider said. He turned and stared at Lizzie Bat. "She doesn't love *me*." And he kept his gaze leveled at Lizzie Bat, saying nothing more, only giving the slightest raise of an eyebrow. "Promise me you won't follow me inside."

"I promise."

And with that, Spider left her and went to the old Victorian, to the place his family owned but stayed out of, so he could steal a glass eye from a ghost.

The metal doorknob did not rattle loudly when turned. The front door neither creaked nor cracked when pulled open. Spider stepped inside and the door shut like a whisper. He held his breath and believed that the house did the same.

To his left, the stairwell to the second floor. Ahead of him, the hallway to the kitchen. To the right, the living-room entry and, closest to the kitchen, the dining room. He stepped forward into the dim silence. Eyes darted to the stairwell and to the doorways, to the shadows and the corners, looking for what he did not want to see. Silence all the way. And he froze.

A glass eye beside the kitchen sink.

From where the eye sat on the counter, it would have *seen* him enter the house, would have *watched* him coming down the hall. That it looked at him, Spider had no doubt. He grabbed the eye and ran from the home.

Lizzie Bat bounced excitedly across the street. "Did you get it?" she said.

Spider leaned on his friend and allowed himself to breathe. He trembled, but he was grinning. "I got it," he said, and he held his hand out to her.

"Is this a joke?" she said.

Hairs on the back of his neck tingled. Weightlessness came to his stomach. "What the fuck?" He held nothing at all.

Lizzie looked over his shoulder towards the house. "Maybe

you dropped it?"

"He took it," Spider said. "I don't know how but he took it back inside." Spider marched to the house with a resolve he lacked the first time.

"Forget it," said Lizzie Bat.

Spider walked on without a word or even so much as a glance. Up the steps and through the door, he returned to the silence. And he laughed. "I know what you're doing," he said, as he entered the house. "But you can't hurt me anymore." He climbed the stairwell to the second floor, stomping his feet as he went. The front door closed, quietly, by itself.

The bathroom door stood open, the only opened door on the second floor. And the glass eye looked at Spider from atop the toilet. He grabbed it and stuffed the eye into the pocket of his jeans. Then, before he turned to leave, he heard the front door open and shut. He called out, "I told you not to follow me." But no one answered and Spider suddenly wished he hadn't said anything at all. The footsteps sounded heavy, like a man's.

"Hello?" said Spider, much more quiet this time. Someone walked downstairs, back and forth from the kitchen to the front door. Footsteps to the dining room, then to the living room, as if looking for something. Spider backed away from the bathroom door and said, "Grandpa?"

The footsteps stopped.

Hide and seek, Spider thought, *that's what Grandpa used to call it.* Spider held his breath, like he had done so many times before. Then, the footsteps again, but now they came from the stairwell. Louder than before and getting closer. Spider pressed against the far wall of the bathroom and watched the open doorway.

Footsteps on the landing, walking down the hall, coming towards the bathroom. Now the steps were at the door and in the room but there was no one there. Spider took a sharp breath. The footsteps stopped and a voice whispered, "I found you."

Spider launched himself off the wall and out of the bathroom. Slick hardwood flooring slipped him up but he didn't spill over. The boy scrambled down the steps, wrenched open the front door and leaped from the porch, tumbling into the yard. Lizzie Bat ran to him and he startled when she touched him.

Spider jumped to his feet and pointed to the house, laughing madly. "Fuck you," he said. "I beat you." And he reached into his pocket. His *empty* pocket. "You gotta be fucking kidding me."

"Forget about it," said Lizzie Bat. "Let it go."

"No." Spider pulled away from her. "It's just a game." He looked back and forth, from Lizzie Bat to the house. "It's just a goddamned game of hide and seek," said Spider. "And there's only one last place to hide in there."

"I'm coming with you," said Lizzie Bat.

"Absolutely not," said Spider. "No way, no how." He shook his head in protest. "This is the last time, Lizzie, I swear. I just have to find him one last time." And once more, Spider made for the front door.

"Him?" Lizzie Bat cocked her head. "Are you stealing a glass eye or a ghost?"

Spider pushed open the door. "I'm not sure which one it is," he said, and looked back at her. "I just know I want to be rid of it."

The basement was only accessible from the kitchen. Spider kept his head down and walked softly. A switch by the basement door turned on the only lightbulb down there. Little light offered, but plenty of shadows cast in all directions. The stairs were roughed in and unfinished, the flight too narrow, and each step a crackling moan. No one could sneak into this basement. No one could sneak out.

Grandpa Whistle's house had been built ages ago. Stones from Mischief River had been used for the foundation. No finished flooring in the basement, only dirt and shale. A dilapidated workbench nearest the stairwell and, on the floor beside that bench, an old rusted hatch that once opened up to a deep well. A faded and cracked door on the far side of the basement lead to what had been a canning room. Spider stood on the last step and surveyed everything. Nothing out of place, no thin movements among the shadows.

"I'm finished with you," Spider said, as he crossed to the canning room, which yawned a cloud of dust when opened the door and sounded like a broken bone. The glass eye sat on one of the meager shelves inside. Spider took the eye and a voice called from behind, "Can you help me?" and Spider jumped and stumbled backwards.

"I'm sorry," said the voice. "Do you think you can come here and help me up?"

Spider couldn't bring himself to blink and his heart pounded in his chest. He peered across the basement. Nothing out of place, no thin movements among the shadows, but now the rusted hatch sat open. "I've been lost in these tunnels for ages." The voice, a child's voice, came from inside the well in the floor.

Spider shut the canning room door behind him and squeezed the glass eye. He stood a good, safe distance from the edge of the well. "I can't see you," he said.

"I can see you just fine."

"I'm going to get a flashlight," Spider said.

"Please, don't do that. The light will be too bright. You don't want to blind me, do you?"

Spider took a single step closer to the well. "How did you get down there?"

"I'm playing hide and seek," said the voice. Scratching sounds like fingers in dirt, fingernails across rock, like they are climbing up out of the dark. "I'm playing hide and seek with Grandpa Whistle and we *found* you."

A voice inside Spider's head, removed from regular idle thoughts, told him to run. And it only had to tell him once.

Spider raced across the dirt floor towards the stairs, and the canning room door on the far corner of the room exploded open. Spider hit the second step and from of the corner of his eye he saw a gray man running out of the darkness after him. Spider bounded two steps at a time, screaming all the way.

Spider lunged from the basement into the kitchen. He slammed against the counter, then pushed off and scrambled for the hallway. He never looked over his shoulder, not once, never needed to, because he knew exactly what Grandpa Whistle's eyes looked like and he did not wish to see them ever again. And, he almost made it.

Outside, Spider gave the glass eye to Lizzie Bat. "Only something I could steal," he said through tears.

"That you'd never dream of taking," Lizzie Bat said. "I'll always love you for that."

"You should go," he said.

"Not going to walk me home?" she said. "Not very gentlemanly."

"We'll catch up," he said. "Eventually."

Lizzie Bat smiled. "You and your secrets."

Spider looked back at the house and wondered what really lie at the bottom of that basement well and the possibility that Grandpa Whistle may have played much worse games with other children. He looked at the house and felt crushed by the horrible truth of it all. Their game of hide and seek would never be over.

"What are you looking at?" asked Lizzie Bat.

Spider, seeing himself in the second-floor window of the old Victorian house, said, "Hell."

III.

In the nighttime, under moonlight, Owl's shovel bit into the ground. Black earth splashed the time-worn tombstone like an arterial spray. A cut most unkind, this lacerated place of rest, a grave in violation. *Who am I?* she thought. And then, she remembered what Lizzie Bat had said.

"I want each of you to steal something for me." Lizzie Bat's words burned brightly in the recesses of Owl's mind. "Something only you could steal. But something you'd never dream of taking."

Owl's thoughts had immediately wandered to stories her great-grandpa used to tell, when she was still a little girl and he was still alive and she yet loved him. He'd been an undertaker since he was a young man, his first and only job. For a spell, he had been the *only* undertaker in October, Illinois. "I've seen more dead bodies than you can shake a stick at," he was fond of saying. But there was one body he never forgot and he never missed a chance to tell the tale. "Prettiest woman I ever laid eyes on, even murdered like she was," he'd say. "Goddamn that Hop Holloway and his nasty business." The old man would stare off and you just knew he was seeing her again, and then he'd get into the whole ghastly affair.

"Annamarie, one of three, dead at Hop's hands on Halloween," great-grandpa said. "Silly song the children used to sing."

"Morbid stuff, if you ask me," said Owl's mother.

"Lots of silly stuff is born out of morbidity," great-grandpa said, and then smiled at young Owl. "Silly things make life less scary."

Owl remembered crawling into great-grandpa's lap and resting her head to his chest, asking, "Why did he kill the pretty lady?"

"Because Hop loved her and Annamarie didn't love him back."

"How do you know he loved her?"

"Because he bought a very beautiful, very expensive necklace for her."

"How do you know she didn't love him?"

"Because she refused to take the necklace from him."

"But how do you know that?"

"Because that's what he used to strangle her to death."

"That's terrible," said young Owl. "I hope he got caught."

"They caught him, alright, the very next day and then they hung him up," said great-grandpa. "Last public hanging in October, I do believe."

"What ever happened to the necklace?" asked Owl's mother.

Great-grandpa let her question sit heavy for a few silent moments, save the odd clicking sound he made with his mouth. He shifted uncomfortably in his chair. "Nobody ever asked," he said, sounding annoyed. "Not one time in all these years."

"If you didn't want people to ask," Owl's mother said, "then maybe it isn't a story you ought to be telling."

He plucked Owl from his lap and stood her on the floor. Even though she was very young, Owl understood that their relationship was about to change forever. And though he was answering her mother's question, great-grandpa looked directly into Owl's eyes. "That necklace went to the grave with Annamarie, I made sure of it." He leaned down and pulled a cigar out of one of his socks. "God forgive me, but she didn't love me either, and I guess I was feeling spiteful." He walked out of the house to smoke on the back porch. He stayed outside through dinner and eventually left without saying goodbye.

Owl never sat on great-grandpa's lap ever again. She refused to go to his funeral. Memories of him were left to wither, and she rarely gave him a second thought as the years passed. Until, that is, Lizzie Bat asked Owl to steal something, something she would never dream of taking.

In the nighttime, under moonlight, Owl found herself walking home. Black earth caked her boots and splattered her jeans up to the knees. *Where am I going?* she thought. *Where have I been?* And then, she reached up to her throat and felt the very beautiful, very expensive necklace.

Owl, pleased and pleasantly tired, aching but energized, stepped out of the shadows and into the vacant street. At this dark and empty hour, the boulevard looked more like a corridor in some impossible house. Or, in some great and cavernous castle in which Owl ruled as a lonely princess—*no*—as a queen. No cars would streak by, not now. No passersby to gawk and wonder what business the queen attended in the present pitch. Occasional streetlights made for elegant torches as she passed and, in the distance, they were as a series of bonfires leading her home, a kind of sympathetic magic. She held her head high and sashayed, humming a song to herself, and she kept to the center of the road, in this fashion.

She cut quickly across town and looked forward to sneaking back into the house and getting some rest. Minutes away, and still so very dark. But the warm air and the sweet smell and the silence of the dark city made the trek all the more agreeable, almost romantic, so she didn't mind.

Owl had almost made it past all the crammed, downtown businesses when she noticed a man following her. *Who could that be at this hour?* she thought, and she stopped for a moment to get a better look, but he stopped too. She stood, not quite panicking, in front the Holbein & Younger Lawfirm, which would put the stranger about three businesses away, the Bartholomew Fair pharmacy. *I should run,* she thought. *He won't catch me.*

"Annamarie, one of three, dead at my hands on Halloween," said the dark stranger. "But you aren't Annamarie."

Run, she thought. And to her horror, that's what the dark stranger did. Her scream shattered the surrounding silence. Terror acted as guiding light, now, beconing her home, turning streetlights into passing stars and she into a comet hurtling to the distant atmosphere of safety.

Just before dawn, moonlight waning, Owl ran for her life and the dark stranger followed. The very beautiful, very expensive necklace cracked against her collar bones and raked across her skin. Owl glanced over her shoulder and with a sickening shock she saw that he was right behind her. His eyes sunken, tongue bloated and black and hanging from his mouth, and his neck raw and broken. Hop Holloway reached out for her. *Not for me,* she thought. *The necklace.*

She reached up and frantically felt for the clasp. For the briefest of moments, the necklace tightened around her neck like a vise. In the next moment, she felt it slip away. And when she looked over her shoulder, this time, there was nothing and no one behind her. But she kept on running, all the same, and did not stop until she got home. She snuck in through her bedroom window, climbed into bed, and fell into deepest sleep.

The smell of brewed coffee cut through her room. Her father, unseen, lumbered through the house and out the door on his way to work. Then, a hint of eggs and the grease of bacon, the familiar sizzle of their cooking. The clanging spring of a toaster. The sun had been up for a spell when her mother called out from across the house, "Breakfast is ready." Early-morning talk shows barked from the television in the living room.

Owl lay in her bed, exhausted, as one startled awake from uneasy dreams. She tossed her filthy clothes into the back of her closet and dressed for the day. Her head hurt almost as much as her legs, and she didn't sit at the dining table as much as she fell into the chair. A plate of hot food waited for her. Mother sat on the couch in the next room, idly watching the television and sipping coffee, as she did every morning. Owl winced and rubbed her temples. "Something's wrong," she said. Her eyes shut tight and she had the sensation of falling backwards, falling into someone else's arms, and then Owl ceased to exist.

"Did you sleep okay?" asked Owl's mother.

"Dreamed I was choking," the young woman said. Her words were barely more than a mumble. "I was buried alive. A young girl saved me."

"Oh," said Owl's mother. "That's too bad." She lifted the remote and turned up the volume on the television.

Breakfast smelled good and looked delicious, and the meal must have been extraordinary, because when she looked at her plate, all the food had already been eaten. Aftertaste in place of memory, she couldn't recall taking a single bite. Fork and knife sat crossed on the empty plate. She rested her hands in her lap. *Where am I?* she thought. And she looked about the room for a mirror or a bit of mail or photographs, anything to anchor her to what was happening or who she was or where she had been taken. She spied a woman who sat on a couch in the next room, her back to her.

"Who are you?" the young woman asked, but her meek inquiry was no match for the loud color television. She grabbed the knife and stood up. "Who are you?" she said, louder this time.

The woman shook her head. She sipped a coffee, then gingerly placed the oversized mug atop the table beside her. She shifted so that she could throw an arm over the couch and face the young woman. A brow furrowed in annoyance gave way to something more like surprise, and the woman's eyes practically bulged out of her head.

"Where did you get that beautiful necklace?" asked the woman.

Annamarie reached up, and screamed. She kept screaming as she brought the knife down, over and over. She was screaming when the police arrived, and screaming when they took her away.

IV.

Many decisions led to Katherine's death, and many of those decisions were completely beyond her control, but her choice to interview for a job at Trick R Treats was hers and hers alone. And, she did this in secret, a surprise for Lizzie Bat, a surprise for all of them. After all, what need would there be in breaking into Trick R Treats if one of them worked there? Kat intended to remove the risk, to keep her friends safe, to supply an alibi and, hopefully, a key.

Of course, Lizzie Bat had warned Kat about Lawrence Ragsdale. He was a creep, she had said. He only employed girls, implying he was some kind of predator or, at the least, a sex pest. According to Lizzie Bat, he was—and Kat snickered at the thought of it—a *vampire*.

She did not know, when she woke in the early hours, that the day would be her last. Anything she did, anyone she saw, was for the final time. She marched towards death in innocence.

"I'll be late coming home today," Kat told her father over breakfast.

He sipped his coffee and straightened his tie. "You promised to make dinner," he said.

She picked at her microwaved waffle. "I can grab something on the way home," she said.

Her father lowered his glasses and leaned toward her. "With what money?" he asked.

She sat back in her seat. "I've got some cash."

He frowned. Then, her father took a drink of coffee before getting up and walking to the sink. He let the water run for a couple seconds and then rinsed out his cup. "You're supposed to be using that money to buy lunch," he said.

"It's a job interview."

He shut off the water and turned towards her, folding his arms. A deep sigh escaped him and he said, "I thought I said *no jobs* till school's over. You don't need the distraction." He checked his watch.

"It's just a seasonal thing," she said. "Trick R Treats is hiring extra staff for the month."

He checked his watch, again. "I'm going to be late," he said. "I want you home after school. You're going to *make* dinner, not buy it. Do we understand each other?"

She stared at her lap and softly said, "It's just a few weeks."

"Is there something wrong with your hearing?" He stomped across the room and slammed his hand on the table. "Do I need to take you to see a doctor?"

Kat fought back tears. "No," she said, pitifully

"Then what did I say?" he said. "And you better fucking look at me when I'm talking to you."

"Fine." Kat looked at him. She let the tears roll down her face. "I'll make your goddamned dinner."

He lifted her clean out of her chair and pinned her against the wall. "You want to act like your mother, then I'll treat you like your mother." He let her go and she slid to the floor. "You smart off to me again and you'll regret it, believe me."

She waited till he was out the door and then she allowed herself to sob uncontrollably. She curled into a ball and called out to her mother. The house offered nothing but silence and brief solitude. Her body felt impossibly heavy but she pushed herself up and got to the bathroom where she washed her face and put in a few eyedrops.

Kat dawdled but managed to get to school just before the bell rang. She knew her friends would have been waiting for her, but she wasn't ready to see anyone. She hated crying in front of people. And then, there would be questions to avoid. She decided, during the first hour of classes, that it was probably best if she avoided them altogether. At least, until after the job interview. So, when final period rolled around, she ducked out early and hurried to her car, only to find out she hadn't been quite as quick and as clever as she hoped.

Lizzie Bat leaned against the driver's door, smoking, one hand buried in the pocket of her tattered jeans. "First, Spider. Then, Owl. And now, you," she said. "It's almost like you guys are avoiding me on purpose."

"What's up with Spider and Owl?" asked Kat.

"If I knew where they are, I'd ask them." Lizzie Bat smirked and pointed. "What's up with you?"

"Nothing is up."

"Oh, okay," Lizzie said. "You're just cutting class and rushing out to your car like you do every day of the week. Got it."

"You're impossible."

"I'm not the one dodging friends and sneaking out of school."

"Something we'd never dream of taking, right?" Kat said, defensively. "That's what you asked us to steal, so that's what I'm going to get you."

Lizzie Bat cocked her head to one side and sized up her friend. "I *knew* you were up to something," she said, grinning.

"I want out of this town as badly as you do, believe me." Kat stepped close to Lizzie Bat. "I want to get as far away from here as I can." She reached out and, gingerly, borrowed the cigarette, licking her lips before taking a drag.

"You never smoke," said Lizzie Bat. "Are you okay?"

"Can I tell you something?" said Kat. She handed the cigarette back to Lizzie Bat. "You were the first person to make me smile when we moved here, and I hadn't smiled in a long time."

"You can talk to me."

"I want to," she said. "And I will, but I just need time."

"I'm here," said Lizzie Bat. "I'll always be here." She held out her arms and Kat went to her. They hugged, and Kat rested her head on Lizzie Bat's shoulder.

"Thank you."

"Don't mention it," said Lizzie Bat. "Now, where are you running off to?"

Kat studied Lizzie Bat's face. Hazel eyes turned gold in afternoon light. Wild hair fell over the beat-up cardigan, it's green color clashing against a purple t-shirt. Kat briefly touched her own lips before sweetly smiling. And then, she offered her parting words to her dearest friend, "That's a surprise."

Downtown ran along the riverfront, not quite a five-minute's drive from the high school. Antique stores and coffee shops with their baked goods and locally-owned curios dotted Main Street. And, for one month of the year, Trick R Treats crawled out of its slumber and opened its massive double-door entrance to the public. The thoroughfare would remain crowded until November, when Trick R Treats went back to sleep.

Kat found street parking a few doors down. A small crowd gathered near the storefront in the hopes of seeing the goings on within, but black drapes offered only slivers of a sneak preview. Trick R Treats storefront display changed every day and, closer to five, those drapes would be pulled away in time for the evening's open hours. There'd be lines of people waiting to get in and, though the lines may die down over time, the store would be busy right up until it closed on midnight, October 31st.

The doors did not budge when pulled. Kat glanced at the people milling about either side of her and rolled her eyes. "Of course," she said to herself, and reached out to knock—

But it opened, as if in anticipation. The crowd loosed a few surprised gasps as Kat slipped inside. "Lucky girl," said someone in the crowd, and then the door shuttered and locked and the outside world was gone.

"He's expecting you," said the dark-eyed blonde who let Kat inside.

"Thanks," Kat said with a nod. "Didn't you used to go to October High?"

"He's in his office," said the blonde, motioning to the red door at the back of the store. The office entrance stood as a fiery beacon within the shop's black interior, like a red eye in the dark. Girls in every aisle set up merchandise. A trio of young women prepped displays at the storefront. A few stood atop ladders and hung decorations from the ceiling. More than a few familiar faces, though Kat had a hard time placing them. The blonde said, "Don't keep him waiting."

Kat turned to respond to her but she had already sauntered away. Kat raised a hand in the blonde's direction, but shrugged her shoulders and went on her way. Not a single one of the employees acknowledged Kat as she hurried to the office.

The air felt punishingly cold in Trick R Treats. She shivered in front of the red door and quickly checked her watch. Father would be home soon and dinner would not be ready. "Don't just stand out there shaking," said a man's voice from inside. Kat glanced back to see everyone had stopped their work. They all watched her. "Come in, come in," he said. And, slightly unnerved but not yet alarmed, in she went.

A desk and a few chairs made up a bulk of the office. No windows to speak of, but a computer monitor sat to the side, running four different security cameras. Every angle of the store accounted for in grainy black and white video. Lawrence Ragsdale motioned to the seat opposite him and said, "Take a load off."

"Thank you," said Kat, and then she settled in. She offered a smile to the man across the table and he returned with one of his own. He stared, and smiled, but only stared and smiled. She kept her own smile going as long as she felt able but the exchange quickly entered uncomfortable territory, so she laughed, nervously. And he laughed too. Unable to meet his gaze any longer, Kat turned her attention to her lap, to the floor. Lawrence Ragsdale continued to say nothing to her, but he stared and he smiled and he stared and he smiled.

Kat fidgeted and checked the time and knew her father would be home soon. She said, "Is this some kind of joke?" And when the man did not answer, Kat stood to leave and screamed when she turned around. The familiar blonde stood behind her and blocked the closed door to the office. "I'm sorry," said Kat. She placed a palm to her forehead in embarrassment. "I didn't hear you come in."

"Don't keep him waiting," said the blonde. She raised an eyebrow, then looked in his direction. She winked before turning to Kat. "Well?" she said. "What are you waiting for?"

A desk and a few chairs made it *look* like an office. A few props could set any scene, not unlike the Halloween decorations lining the aisles of the store. The lack of windows felt, suddenly, like a trap. Lawrence Ragsdale, still smiling, pointed to the seat opposite him and said, "Sit down." Kat stood frozen in place until the blonde came up from behind her and, with considerable strength, took Kat by the shoulders and directed Kat to the chair before pushing her down in it.

"I should leave," said Kat. She looked back and forth to the blonde and the man. "I have to make dinner."

Lawrence Ragsdale leaned back in his chair and said, "No."

"I'm sorry, but I really should go," said Kat. "I'll get into trouble if I don't go."

Lawrence waved his hands in rebuttal. "We'd love to have you join the Trick R Treat family," he said. "We'd love to have you." He pointed up and smiled, but not like before, this was the smile of a madman. Kat felt her stomach drop.

The walls inside the office were painted black, like the store. Kat hadn't noticed just how high up those walls went. She trembled near uncontrollably when she saw the ceiling. She collapsed from the chair when balance failed her and scrambled away but there was nowhere to go, no place to which she could escape. They were all up there, upside down and smiling and watching, every employee she had passed on the way to the office. Skin like snow in moonlight and black eyes that seemed to shine and parted lips, red as rubies.

And their teeth.

"Kat, can I tell you something?" said Lawrence. He snapped and whistled to get her attention. "I know what you're doing, what your plan is—sorry—*was*."

"My father's going to be so mad."

"You thought you'd waltz in here and get a job and steal from *me*?"

"He'll hit me," she said.

"Like he hit your mother."

"How do you know about my mother?"

"I know your mother's dead and that you lie to your friends. I know lots of things," he said. "Just like I know you're going to love it here."

The world seemed to fall out from beneath her. Lawrence Ragsdale, his rictus grin seemingly lifted from a jack-o-lantern, lurched to the top of his desk like an animal. They were crawling down the walls now, all of the girls.

"Oh, and Kat? Try not to scream," he said. "It's bad for business." He reached over and turned off the light.

But she could still see their eyes.

V.

Grandma Rae lived in the October Memorial Care Center, though Lizzie Bat did not know with any certainty whether the choice had been that of her mother or her father. She could only suspect. Shadow Mother had, after all, never gotten along with Grandma Rae. Their relationship only became more strained as Grandma Rae slipped further into dementia. *Out of sight*, Lizzie Bat thought, *out of mind.*

Lizzie Bat wasted time that day till Shadow Mother left the house. To run some errands, check on some things, this is what she told her daughter, but before she left, she made sure that she said, "Stay out of the attic. Stay out of his things."

Lizzie Bat watched her leave, then ran to her bedroom and picked up clothes and made her bed and made sure the glass book was hidden, not under her pillow, where Shadow Mother might just look, but underneath the box spring was where she hid the book.

Then, on her bike and on the road.

Out of sight.

Out of mind.

To grandmother's house we go.

She thought it an awful betrayal, being kept in a place like the Care Center, waiting for death, letting perfect strangers take care of you until it happened. She wondered if many people saw that very same betrayal in their immediate future. She certainly saw it in her own. Who wanted to take care of a ghost?

People like Grandma Rae had graves waiting to be filled at Lovejoy or Oakwood Cemetery, with a headstone to be provided by Batson Memorial, no less. She wondered where her grave would be. She wondered where it waited, the open mouth with its hunger only for her.

Sun had gone from overhead to setting beyond trees to the west. Orange and red became pink and purple in quick succession, and soon after a deep blue stretched from one horizon to the other. Lizzie Bat realized she hadn't taken a breath.

A ghost, she thought, as she walked into the building, *wearing a dead man's red scarf, walking into a home filled with people waiting to die.* She laughed at her own morbid humor.

"I'm here to see Mrs. Rachel Batson."

The receptionist raised her eyebrows.

"Visiting hours are almost over, young lady. Why don't you come back tomorrow when you'll have more time?"

Lizzie Bat eyed the woman's name tag. "Well, Nancy, the trouble is, I'm here because my mother asked me to stop by. I'm sure you know her. Gloria Batson? Anyway, Gloria wanted me to stop in and see how her mother is doing. I only need to check in for just one minute. Gloria, my mother, she wants me to call her as soon as I do. You've got to know Gloria Batson." She leaned across the desk and whispered, "Kind of a pain in the ass if you ask me."

The receptionist laughed. "Yes, I know Gloria."

"I rode a bike all the way across town to get here." Lizzie Bat clasped her hands together and thrust them toward the receptionist. "Please, don't make me beg."

"I tell you what, I'll let you see Miss Rae, but you gotta be quick and then you gotta be gone. Sign in on the sheet. And you be sure to tell Gloria that we take good care of her momma."

Lizzie Bat hurried towards Grandma Rae's room. A hint of brewed coffee cut through the smell of disinfectant. Nancy must've needed help getting through the nightshift. These aromas did not abate the septic odor of humans wasting away. She couldn't shake the idea that this *was* a kind of cemetery, with people in place of headstones. She did not want this.

Grandma Rae's room sat in darkness, save the little bit of

clarity creeping through the blinds, an errant glimmer of a nearby streetlight. Lizzie Bat did not dare turn on the overheads. She left the door to the room ajar, so as to let in a little of the glow from fluorescent hallway lighting. She barely opened her mouth. "Grandma?" she said, in an absolute whisper, as if her voice could be more abrasive than dying alone with a damaged mind, in a place that was little more than a waiting room for the grave.

"Grandma Rae, it's me," she said. "I'm sorry I never come to visit." She sat on the edge of the bed.

"I know." Grandma Rae's voice was so soft that Lizzie Bat worried she'd imagined it. "I know."

Grandma Rae sat up. "I know," she said again, and reached out to touch Lizzie Bat's face. She smiled. It was a toothless grin. Her wide eyes looked in Lizzie Bat's direction but not at her. Through her.

Searching.

"I'm leaving," Lizzie Bat said, "and I'm never coming back. I can't do this anymore. But I wanted to tell you that I love you."

"Elizabeth." Grandma Rae stopped smiling. Her eyes narrowed. Her brow furrowed. She squeezed her hand. "I know." The corners of her mouth pulled down. She cried. "I know."

Lizzie Bat pulled her grandmother close and held her. It wasn't the forgetting that was painful. It was remembering.

Grandma Rae pulled away from her. She was lost again, and smiling.

Lizzie Bat said, "I can't do this anymore." She stood, Grandma Rae's eyes locked on hers. She mouthed *I love you* to the old woman.

One last "I know," and Grandma Rae acquiesced into her peaceful darkness.

Lizzie Bat watched the old woman sleep. Grandma Rae's breathing sounded labored and the struggle broke Lizzie Bat's heart. She sat in the dark, telling the sleeping woman she loved her, over and over, until the collar of her t-shirt was soaked with tears. She kissed her grandmother on the forehead, one final time.

Lizzie bat collected herself, said goodnight to Nancy the receptionist, and she hurried out the door. She could not bring herself to look back at the building. She rode her bike, for the last time, back home.

She snuck in through the back of the house, closed the door, and listened for her mother, walking as softly as she could, walking like a whisper would, until she heard a noise. A shatter and crack and grind and a chew and a tinkling like discordant notes, the type of song sung by beads on plates or marbles in a jar. Lizzie Bat followed the sound and, soon, candlelight creeping from the dining room, where Shadow Mother had arranged a candlelight dinner for herself.

Shadow Mother did not look up as she sopped up what looked like a brittle stew. "The police came looking for you," she said, slurping and chewing.

"What are you eating?" asked Lizzie Bat, not hearing her mother's words.

"I suppose you haven't heard from Owl in a while."

"What are you eating?"

"Or Spider." Shadow Mother rose, still chewing, blood flowing from her mouth, running down her front, and blood pooled in the plate before her. Candlelight cast a weak luminance but offered dozens of brilliant garnet glows, a thousand tiny reflections bouncing off of broken bits of bitten glass. Shadow Mother had found his book, and she ate it.

His book.

"Seems your friend Owl killed her mother."

His words.

"And Spider's body was found in the basement of a house on Christian Hill."

His voice.

Shadow Mother swallowed and the labored gulp sounded like brushing glass into a garbage can. She lightly dabbed the corners of her mouth. Then, she held out an envelope.

"I wanted to wait until you were older to give you this," said Shadow Mother. "I thought, perhaps, I could spare you from the truth about your father. There's too much of him in you."

"You took him from me," said Lizzie Bat. "You took his book, his words, his voice."

"Your father took those things when he decided to leave us," said Shadow Mother, and she shook the envelope. "It's all right here in his goodbye."

"He's alive?" said Lizzie Bat, almost hopeful, and she snatched the envelope.

Shadow Mother said, "You treat me like I'm your enemy but I've only ever tried to keep you safe."

"Keep me safe from what?" said Lizzie Bat.

"Death." Shadow Mother gripped Lizzie Bat's arm. "He fed himself to one of his goddamned monsters, you silly girl."

The envelope felt impossibly heavy in Lizzie Bat's hands and the envelope got heavier with each passing moment. She closed her eyes and let the contents slip forth like a sigh. The note unfolded silently.

`I went looking.`

Then, the clock struck twelve and, with those chimes, the day's eyes rolled up into its head and it breathed its last. Halloween's arms opened wide and made impossible promises.

PART 3:
OBLIVION IN A WHISPER

By the time you read this, I will be in the belly of a beast at the bottom of black waters. If you ever want to visit, then the Mischief River is my grave. And, if you choose not to visit, then I understand and respect that choice.

A year ago, I was diagnosed with early-onset Alzheimer's disease. I had my suspicions but I kept these to myself. Forgotten keys became forgotten names and dates and trouble with everyday tasks. I took time off to write my book, at least that's what I told everyone. Truth is, I had to get away from folks. I got scared of being found out, I suppose.

I can feel this separation between who I was and who I am becoming, and that space ripples within a profound sadness. I do not know the woman I love. I do not know my daughter. I see them in pictures within a house that feels stranger to me with each passing day. I cannot bring myself to reach out and touch them, though I try. If not with my hands, then with my very soul. I can no longer remember my mother and father. It feels like there's a hole in the sky where God used to be. And I am so terribly afraid.

I am honestly terrified.

No one deals well with change, because change—the kind that really matters and affects you—is often emotionally gut-wrenching. I don't think something qualifies as a real change unless it quickens your heart and makes your stomach feel like it is dropping out. That's when you know. No one wants to feel like that, and that's why people would rather placate themselves and spend their life being just a little miserable. Change is the only way to abate misery, and a miserable life is change ignored. There is no way out of this.

You love a man who is already gone. I am a stranger writing to you on his behalf. I believe he loved you with all his heart. Love is what kept him going for as long as he could. But, even love has become difficult, and that breaks my heart because I fear it will break your heart. If I am fated to hurt the ones I love, then I only wish to do it this one time.

Love is a dog at your feet, demanding your meal. Love is that silent hesitation when you first notice bright stars crack through clouds on a black night. Love is a memory of light reflecting on snow. A contagious smile. Electric sensation of touch reciprocated. The cold finality of unmovable stone. The face you are slowly forgetting. The smell of rain on hot pavement. A night without shadows. Love is an animal screaming in the dark.

I am tired of being scared and screaming in the dark. A change must be made, and I must make it while I still have the senses to approach that change with some modicum of bravery. I do hope you can find it in your heart to forgive me.

I.

This is how the end begins on Halloween:

Darkness, darkness, everywhere. A new moon reflects this darkness from the cauldron of the infinite, high above the raven clouds that sweep unseen, they roll across the sunless earth like acrid smoke from a fire raging in the pitch. And nearly everyone's asleep in this darkness, this tenebrous sea of dreams.

Minutes after midnight, Lizzie Bat reads her father's letter. Then, she falls to her knees and screams. Her broken heart causes all the windows in the house to explode and the city briefly loses power.

And there is such a silence, no answer to her cries, and the black waters of Mischief River reflect the entirety of the dark universe stretched before its plutonium shores, reflect an infinity, unknowable and never ending, reflect the empty eye sockets of the celestial heavens, and Lizzie Bat retreats below the black waters because even this reflection is too bright, plummets beyond the cemetery at the bottom of her heart, because darkness is not dark enough. She yearns for something somehow darker, and holds in her heart that this perfect darkness is attainable, yearns for a grave, her grave, and gives this grave a name.

Oblivion.

"I can't do this anymore."

Darkness, darkness, everywhere.

"I can't do this anymore."

October 31st is born on the black wings of grief. No one awake knows it is the beginning of the end. No one asleep dreams it is the last day.

Halloween's time has come.

***

Daniel Batson didn't just die, like she had been told, he did not simply disappear and die, not the first time. He . . . *went looking.* But when he died the second time, his death was at the hands of Shadow Mother, who burned his books, burned his words, burned his voice until it smoldered and smoked like a soul escaping. Shadow Mother never cried, she *never* cried, even after he died for a third time. Lizzie Bat could not save him, would never save him, not from Shadow Mother, and not from himself. Daniel Batson died, and died forever, and the finality of his death threatened to crush Lizzie Bat.

No one came to comfort or called out to calm her nerves and Shadow Mother, unmoving, remained. A whisper, then, a voice at the bottom of a deep well, crawled across Lizzie Bat's skin and tickled the fine hairs along her body before washing over her completely. "I need you to see me." Eyes softly glowed, a subtle phosphorescence, a creature of deepest sea, enticing prey with all the colors of the rainbow. Shadow Mother looked at Lizzie Bat and then through her flesh and through muscle and through bone and through the soft tissue of her brain and settled inside her mind. Her dark light burned bright and lit up the interior of Lizzie Bat's subconscious.

Before her remained Shadow Mother, but in her mind appeared her mother from before her father's death, her real mother, the mother of her childhood memories, though this mother stood incomplete, a ghostly but not ghastly form, like humming notes to a song half-forgotten or a photograph faded by time. She had form but her features, her face, streaked and warped, except the right eye. The right eye looked perfect.

"I'm not going to hurt you," said the mother in Lizzie Bat's mind.

"She's a grand liar," whispered Shadow Mother. "Do not trust her."

The mother of childhood memories snapped back. "Shut up,

damn you, and mind your own business."

Shadow Mother hissed but cowered, retreating from the stinging light of words from her better self.

"She called you a grand liar," said Lizzie Bat.

"We are all liars," said the mother of childhood memories. "Maybe *grand* is a bit much."

"Is this a dream?" asked Lizzie Bat. "This must a dream. This has to be a dream, my god, a dream."

"Is not all we see or seem a dream within a dream?" Her perfect eye swirled, a red and black light, forever twisting inward, hypnotic and not unlike drowning. Shadow Mother had called her a liar, but she seemed worse than that. She felt dangerous.

"You are not my mother," said Lizzie Bat.

"I am your mother," she said. "Or, I am as your mother once was."

"Get out of my head."

"My doppelgänger may be a monster but she is not your enemy," said the mother of childhood memories. "She needs your empathy."

"I can never forgive her," said Lizzie Bat. "I can never forget."

"Empathy asks neither forgiveness or forgetting."

"I'm leaving and I am never coming back."

"I will take care of you. I always have, always will. Until you bury me in the grave, and even then, I will be with you," she said. The mother of childhood memories dimmed and the subconscious went dark.

Lizzie Bat held her breath and felt around, running through the recesses of her own mind and memories, looking for any signs of the intruder. So many places to hide. She could be crouched behind the time Lizzie Bat lost her first tooth. She might hide under the dinner where Lizzie Bat laughed so hard at her father that they all cried. The mother of childhood memories was gone and Shadow Mother was all that remained.

Shadow Mother.

Her mother.

Her face.

A warm embrace.

Her smile.

The sound of her voice.

"I am your mother," she said. "Or, I am all that is left."

"What do you want from me?" said Lizzie Bat.

"When I look at you, all I see is your father and it is killing me," said Gloria. "I want you to go away and never return."

Despite the cutting words, Lizzie Bat's animosity seemed to suddenly wash away, as if it had been nothing more than a passing cloud. She wondered how much of the woman was real, and how much of her was a disguise. There had not been a single moment when she and her mother were together, since his death, that Lizzie Bat felt like her mother ever looked *at* her, only *through* her.

"I love you," said Lizzie Bat, unsure of the words escaping her mouth.

A photograph on the wall behind her mother distracted Lizzie Bat and grounded the young woman in a new reality, one without mother or father, a reality where she was alone, no longer tethered to their expectations. She no longer saw mother or father, but two people estranged from her own existence. She saw their pain; she saw her own.

The frame was red, decorated in embossed hearts. Her mother, younger—she was laughing—and with much more color in her hair, she had her arm around a boy in a red scarf. Mother had taken down all the other photos, but left this single snapshot. Not another framed picture of the man anywhere else in the house, except right here. A memorial, but not to him. This memorial was for a love now dead and gone.

It wasn't the forgetting that was painful. It was remembering.

Lizzie Bat said, "Goodbye, Mother." And she meant what she said.

Oblivion.

II.

Trick R Treats stood less than two blocks away. The skies would be dark within the hour, but that didn't bother Lizzie Bat. She was better equipped for the night. The world was never dark enough for her, anyway.

Downtown October rumbled with steady traffic, lots of cars driving north, out of town. Couples and sightseers headed up the winding road along the Mischief River to watch the sunset. Groups of motorcycle riders roared by, always in groups, covered in leather, heading to some of the bars that peppered the downtown strip.

Music played in the distance. Some crooner belted out *Hallelujah* at the top of his lungs, while westering clouds streaked with shades of purple that signaled oncoming night. Closer to the horizon, those purple clouds became soaked with red and orange. The air chilled and the smell of distant fireplaces spoke of winter months to come. October always looked prettier in the dark.

Lizzie Bat ached with loneliness. No mother or father to comfort her. No home to go to. Owl had seemingly become a murderer. Spider was dead. No place left to dream, no place to desire. The city had but one refuge for her, one last person to whom she could turn.

A great stone building loomed before her, like some misplaced castle. Exposure and time had long ago stained its granite face.

People ogled the storefront, the final display of the season. Trick R Treats' oversized entrance, a cupola sitting higher above, looked like something out of an old horror movie. The effect felt very much as if she were about to enter—not a store—but a mausoleum.

The double doors pushed open with relative ease. Cool air escaped in a rush. The hum of air conditioning and busied conversations were as a pleasing static, or an extended whisper, a steady soundtrack for people eager to lose themselves in a costume, lose themselves to dreams, lose themselves to experiences, to escape to their own far-off countries. Halloween spoke to a longing in everyone, to their deeply held desires and secrets, and Halloween begged for these desires and secrets to reveal themselves.

The check-out desk was along the wall and far from the front doors. Lawrence Ragsdale stood behind the cash register. He wore a burgundy cardigan and week-old scruff, the patchy growth of a young man attempting seasoned masculinity or someone who longed for good sleep. The sleeves of his cardigan were pulled up mid-forearm, and there was a hint of tattoo. Not a gray strand anywhere among his shaggy, brown hair. He smiled and waved as Lizzie Bat approached the sales counter. He kept right on smiling as he adjusted his glasses and said, "You're a bit early, aren't you?"

Lizzie Bat let her arms rest on the counter, cupping her hands. "I want to speak to Kat."

"You're not due to rob my store for another"—he checked his watch—"six hours."

"Is she here or not?"

"I knew your dad," Lawrence said. "Daniel, good guy, loved monsters and ghosts and stuff like that. Heard he was writing a book about local legends and cryptids. Such a shame, the way he went. Does that surprise you, that I know all that? I know a lot of things."

Lizzie Bat drummed her fingers on the counter. "I'm going to be perfectly honest," she said. "I don't give a fuck about you."

"Oh, but we care about *you*, Elizabeth Batson," he said, menacingly, and with a flash of teeth. There was the sound of a locking door, and Lizzie Bat turned to see the store empty of customers. All the employees, with their eyes made out of coal and their lips the color of blood, blocked the entrance. "We'd love to have you join the family," he said.

"You don't understand," said Lizzie Bat. "I don't give a fuck about you. I find you exhausting and dull, and if you don't let me speak to Kat—*right now*—I will kill you and all your little friends and I will turn this entire building into cinder and ash."

He leapt onto the counter "Big talk for such a little girl," he said. But, his rictus grin fell.

Lizzie Bat, silently and without a trace of effort, rose from the floor and levitated above Lawrence Ragsdale. "Do you want to die?" she said. "Tell me that you want to die."

"I cannot die," he said, struggling. He blurted out, "But I want to die." He covered his mouth, surprised by his own words.

"Tell me that you want to die," she said, lifting him into the air.

All his power and menace drained away and he whispered, "What are you?"

"Tell me that you want to die."

"I want to die," he said.

A familiar voice from below called out. "Stop."

Lizzie Bat turned to see Kat elbowing past the others, her eyes and lips a ghastly caricature of their former selves. Lizzie Bat tossed Lawrence Ragsdale with all the disinterest of a child for a disappointing toy. "I want to die," he repeated to himself as he crawled away, his employees cooing and doting on him. "I want to die."

Lizzie Bat planted her feet on the floor before her friend. "I told you he was dangerous."

"Something we'd never dream of taking," said Kat. "That's what you asked for."

"Something only you could steal," said Lizzie Bat. "But you didn't steal anything."

"Of course I did," said Kat. "I stole your heart. But I don't want it."

"Please don't say that."

"I never wanted it."

"You don't mean that."

"I don't love you," said Kat. "I will never love you."

Lizzie Bat fell to her knees and what was left of her heart scattered into a cloud of splintered glass a little larger than the entire universe. The force of her scream blew Kat into pieces, as well as anyone else within a few city blocks. Trick R Treats trembled before falling in on itself, a total collapse of such force that the foundation opened up and swallowed the building whole, taking with it several other buildings, until a great crater was all that remained at the center of October. And down, down, down into the dark went Lizzie Bat.

She retreated below black waters
"I wish you were here." (her body shook)
Below the bowels of the earth
"I wish you were here." (her shoulders shook)
Beyond the cemetery at the bottom of her heart
"I wish you were here." (her chest shook)
Because darkness was not dark enough
Oblivion
She called out to her heart
Oblivion
It wasn't the forgetting that was painful. It was remembering.
"Oblivion," she whispered. And, the gravity of her shattered heart forced all of reality to fold in on itself. All that ever was and ever would be ceased to exist outside the boundaries of her heart. Then, after an incalculable passage of time, Elizabeth Batson awoke from strange aeons in her perfect darkness.

Darkness, darkness, everywhere . . .

∞

Reality became cemetery. No sound to hear, not even a whisper. No life sign or any ceremony. Just endless night, like deep black water. Solitude felt like a celebration. Lizzie Bat enjoyed the devastation.

Though, what she did, was it devastation? All life ends in a cemetery. Isn't death the final celebration? And all it took was for her to whisper. Pain, fear, fire extinguished by black water. Escape was its own ceremony.

Your last heartbeat, that's a ceremony. For what is love but a devastation? Good, bad, love is to drown in black water. All love ends in the same cemetery. Time reduces passion to a whisper. Death of love . . . a sorry celebration.

Even love lost trumps no celebration. Ghosts can be their own ceremony. What can end can begin in a whisper. Give them their love, life, their devastation. You choose the path to your cemetery. One can do more than drown in black water.

"Let there be light," she said, "and black water." She said, "Let there be a cemetery." She said, "Let them have their ceremony. They can even have their devastation." All this she commanded in a whisper.

"No witch," she said, "but God," in a whisper. "No dust to read, but I can see water. All of you I'll birth from devastation. And, I may extend a celebration. Halloween, an endless ceremony. Let life be a lovely cemetery."

With her whisper came that celebration.
She spread, like water, the ceremony.
A good devastation . . . and she named this cemetery.

EPILOGUE:
HALLOWEEN FOREVER

On the night of November 1st, God returned to October, Illinois.

Halloween radiated its undying magic. Candlelight and electric decorations, candy corn and costumes, boys and girls who rushed with excitement. She passed through a crowd of hundreds of trick-or-treaters. Fallen leaves crunched underfoot and the smell of fireplaces lingered in the air. People laughed, merrily, and their breath glowed against the coming cold. Sunset cast the last of the day in gold and you could hear the candy wrappers crunching and scraping and when it got dark the neighborhood was awash in purples and reds and oranges and scattered pinpricks of flashlights that slowly moved up and down the sidewalks, a procession of children laughing in the happy shadows.

God looked out and over Her new world, Summer's End, Halloween Forever, the Ghastly and Grim Game. Falling leaves careened, blown by sudden rushes of cool air, like pages of a book lost in the wind or ashes after the fire. God looked upon Her world of night watchmen. They are hollowed out, unawares, and filled with light and they are doomed—*doomed*—to walk till Judgment Day. Not a set date, mind you, but an individual terminus. This is the fate of all Jack-O-Lanterns. But that is not what is important. What is important is that the watchmen once lived and were hollowed out and forced to shine in the dark. They are not wandering souls, alone. They live in each other.

She spied Owl and Spider at a distance. They shared a candy

from Spider's bag and then they shared a kiss. The two of them radiated happiness, and knowing they were happy in Her absence satisfied Her. A flower bloomed in Her cemetery heart. "Happy Halloween," She whispered.

Mischief River's black waters called to Her and She answered. She watched, from high above, the black blood of the earth flow south, cutting the world in two. And then, Her heart skipped a beat. An impossible constellation stood atop the lookout across the river, outside looking in, as always. Going to her, now, would be folly, but God could not resist. She fell, unnoticed, and gathered courage, footsteps as quiet as shadows falling, until She allowed Her presence to be known.

Kat startled. "I'm sorry," she said, regaining composure. "I didn't think anyone would be here."

"It's beautiful at night. October, I mean. Standing here, on top of the remnants of this old bridge, you can see the whole thing. It's quite a view."

"I wasn't born here," Kat explained. "Grew up in California, near mountains, in a dry climate. Can you imagine my surprise when my father moved us here?"

"Do not worry so much about where you end up, but why you will end up there. Maybe that sounds like silly advice, but when it comes to happiness you have to let things get a little corny."

"My mother is so far away," said Kat. "It's an awful pain, absence. I imagine this is how a ghost must feel."

"Not very optimistic."

Kat scoffed, and then said, "Optimism is an evolutionary safeguard—"

"—against reality."

Kat said, "Have we met before?"

"In another life."

"Who are you?"

God looked across the river at the scattering of lights, the little burning signs of life, a sea of shattered recollections. She smiled at the impossible constellation and said, "I'm a ghost."

"I get it," said Kat. "I feel like a ghost sometimes, too."

"Everybody is somebody's ghost."

"Every house is a haunted house," said Kat. "I'll have to remember that."

And God allowed Herself a hint of a smile, both mourning

Kat's absence while being thankful for her memory. The cemetery rested within, and God felt at ease. She asked, "What's that perfume?"

"Lavender," said Kat. "I got it at the mall."

"I love it."

"I like lavender," said Kat.

"It reminds you of your mother."

The collapsing space between them felt fraught with risk. Fitting that they stood at the riverbank, the cemetery of unwanted things. The City of October stood at the banks of the Mischief River as a memorial to a love that never was or ever would be. Unrequited love shambled like a rotting carcass, undying and unfulfilled, a terrifying and indestructible monster.

"I can't do this anymore."

"Leaving all ready?"

Lizzie wants to leave, said Owl. Lizzie always wants to leave.

"Yes," She said, and added, "… finally. There is nothing here for me."

"Are you crying?"

"I can't do this anymore."

God retreated from the bridge by the riverbank, from the black waters of Mischief River, far from the City of October and Halloween Forever, up into the cold reaches of an outer space awash in sunsets and sunrises, all the light in all directions falling and twinkling like broken glass. But no matter how far She went, the impossible constellation could not be escaped. An invisible wall, as thin as a memory, as close as a wink, some melancholy forcefield, the only thing keeping them apart. And, She was terrified of that space, which would never collapse, terrified of how She felt for this electric bloom in a cemetery of Her own creation.

Only loneliness could break this spell.

And so, She pressed on, far from the lonely blue drip in the black ocean without bottom to reach or surface to break, that wet pebble hurtling through infinity, lifeless planets its only friends, a single unimpressive torch lighting its way, because the scariest ghosts are the ones you love.

They never stop haunting you.

ACKNOWLEDGMENTS & AUTHOR'S NOTE

Many thanks to Tracy Robinson and David Taffner for their enthusiasm and very, very early support for this book, as well as their patience, for which I am ever so grateful. Thanks to anyone who beta read bits and pieces of OCTOBER ANIMALS over the last few years. And, thanks to Daniele Serra for his amazing artwork, and to Joe Wieneke for his title treatment.

***

Life is full of *almost* and *never was* and *you imagine what might have been*, and some of these thoughts linger longer than others until they become just as good as memories, memories of moments that never came to pass. At least, not in this life or reality, universe, heartbeat, what have you. And, that's what OCTOBER ANIMALS is about, in a small way.

I started thinking about death as a superpower, the strength of nothingness, the will to create and destroy and to dream better realities from the detritus of lives we've lived. Reinvention is key, I think, to living. And it is never too late to reinvent. Not really. As long as you keep waking up, then there's a chance. And, as long as you keep falling asleep, you get to experience the death of that reinvention. You get to be everything and nothing, over and over, throughout the entire course of your life. If that is not a gift, then I don't know what is.

Maybe we are nothing. Nothing is, after all, all that stretches before our birth and after our death, to say nothing of the need to sleep. We just want to get back to zero, to square one. Clean the slate. Reinvention is our natural state.

We are nothing, and we spend so much time creating a self, and then a facsimile of that, and then a facsimile of that, and so on and so on. And how many of our reinventions live within those we've met? Who are we to these people? Which reinvention is trapped within the confines of another's mind? Have these people, in fact, reinvented us? I can assure you they have, and it has happened over and over again.

Hell is other people, sure, but so is Heaven. There's nothing special in a beating heart. But when it stops, well, that's something. Then you get to live exclusively inside everyone who knew you. If you are very lucky, you'll live within strangers, too.

What a strange and wonderful superpower, death.

About the Author

Nicholas Day is the author of GRIND YOUR BONES TO DUST, NECROSAURUS REX, and AT THE END OF THE DAY I BURST INTO FLAMES. His short fiction is frequently anthologized. He co-owns Rooster Republic Press with Don Noble, where they acquire and produce award-winning horror fiction and poetry.

Currently, he resides in Northern Illinois with his family, and he is always working on new material. You can find more information about him and his work at nicholasdayonline.com